D0186800

SOGGY
the Bear
- who forgot to take care

mabecron books

For those children who have lost
or never had a teddy bear

First published in Great Britain in 2006 by Mabecron Books ltd, 42 Drake Circus, Plymouth Devon PL4 8AB. All rights reserved

Paperback edition 2007

Typeset in Sabon
Designed by Kim Lynch

10 9 8 7 6 5 4 3 2 1

Printed and bound in China

SOGGY
the Bear

Philip Moran

illustrated by
Michael Foreman

A little girl walked with her mother and father along Bamaluz beach. They had driven through the night to their holiday by the sea and were pleased to stretch their legs at last. It was a mysterious, almost secret beach, ringed about by cranky old cottages which seemed to grow up out of the rocks.

While they waited for their holiday cottage to be made ready, the little girl built a sandcastle and placed her favourite teddy bear on top, so he could look at the rocks and the blue-green sea. Suddenly her mother called and the little girl and her father rushed up the steps to see the cottage in which they were to spend their holiday.

The little bear was quite surprised that he had been left alone but he was not really worried. He felt sure that they would come back for him soon and anyway he felt rather important sitting on his sandcastle.

He looked about him. At the end of the beach he saw rock pools warming in the sun.

He looked out to sea and watched the small boats riding gently at anchor, rising slowly up and down as the waves passed under them. It was very peaceful.

'This is the life,' he thought. 'I am a king on my very own castle.'

The sun warmed the little bear's face but every now and then a puff of wind blew through his fur. He looked again at the sea. Now the boats were straining at their moorings as the wind freshened. There seemed to be more water between him and the boats and the beach was smaller.

There was still no sign of his family and the waves were coming ever closer to his castle as the tide came in.

He could hear the swishing of the sea as it reached up the beach and retreated again, tumbling tiny pebbles over and over. The sea grew louder as it came closer but the little bear felt safe on his sandcastle.

He looked around at the beach there was not much of it left. He
looked up at the old houses but nobody looked back at him.

Suddenly the waves were sweeping right up to his castle, swirling around the base and nibbling away at his fortress. Every wave took more of the sand beneath him and slowly the castle began to crumble. He looked desperately up to the old houses. There was no sign of his family.

Another wave hit the castle and it shook as the sand slid away. The castle collapsed beneath him. He fell into the top of the tide and was swept away over the tumbling pebbles and into the sea.

The little bear was not frightened at first. He thought he was swimming… it was a new and exciting experience - soon he could swim to shore and find his family. The tide was now running very strongly out of the bay and he was swept out past an island.

Far above him he could see the men of Coast Watch at their
lookout post but they were not looking for little bears. Suddenly as
the water got very much deeper the little bear began to be afraid.

A cold wind was pushing him ever further from the land. Looking around he could see small boats fishing… but they did not see him. He saw the blue and silver fish darting under him as they went crazy attacking the coloured feathers on the fishermen's hooks. Now the water was soaking into him and he felt very heavy.

It was difficult to keep his face above the waves. He could hardly see the land now, just one strange rock sticking up that looked like a man's head... it was silent and ignored him. The little bear couldn't keep his head above the waves and he looked down through the water.

He was passing over an old wreck of a ship sunk long ago. The bear wondered what had happened to the people on that ship, perhaps they had been saved... who was going to save him?

The land was far away and the bear felt that he would not stay afloat very much longer. His heart began to beat very heavily and he thought this must mean that soon he would sink and never be seen again. He felt very sad that he had not been more careful on the beach… and the pounding of his heart was now getting very loud. He managed one last look upward…

Jack and his grandfather were out fishing. Fed up with catching mackerel, they had moved further offshore to look for the cod. The steering wheel was tied over and the engine was running very slowly, so their fishing boat was circling in the tide as it ebbed down the coast.

The noise the bear heard was not his heart but the slow beat of the engine through the water. He struggled to wave as he drifted past. Jack's grandfather was well known for looking everywhere other than at what he was doing and suddenly he saw the poor little bear lying very low in the water.

Grabbing the gaff he hooked the little bear by the scarf around his neck and hauled him into the boat. 'There Jack,' he said, 'Not often we catch a bear out at sea is it!'

'You are a very lucky bear,' said Jack as he squeezed as much of the water out of him as he could. Then he sat him on the engine box to keep warm until it was time to pull in the lines and go home. Looking at the poor bedraggled bear Grandfather said, 'I don't know where you came from or who you are, so I shall call you "Soggy" from now on.'

Soggy did not care about having a new name... he was just glad to be safe and out of the water, even though the boat was very smelly and there were fish everywhere on the deck and some of them were still looking at him.

When the boat was tied up and
all the fish landed, Jack and
his grandfather took the little bear
home. They gave him a nice warm
soapy bath in a few inches of
water so he was not
frightened this time.

Then they pegged him up in the
bathroom by his ears, which Soggy
thought was a bit much, until he had
dried right through.

The old fisherman carried Soggy carefully up into his living room and placed him in the Rescue Chair with all the other little people and creatures he had found and helped over the years.

Sometimes now Soggy goes with Jack's grandfather to schools to help him tell children about how dangerous it can be if you are not careful on the beach and by the water.
'You must always take care,' Grandfather tells them.
'Remember what happened to Soggy.'

In his new home, Soggy sits with his friends and looks out at the sea. Sometimes he wonders where the little girl is who left him on the beach.

He would like to tell her he is safe and happy
and maybe, one day, she will pass by his window
and they will meet again.